BELVEDERE

by

by GEORGE CRENSHAW

TOR

A TOM DOHERTY ASSOCIATES BOOK

"OLD BUDDY, WE'RE UP AGAINST ONE SMART MOOSE!"

"THEY WERE BOTH IN LOUSY MOODS THIS MORNING."

"'GIVE ME THE WHEEL AND LET'S CHASE THAT SAUCER!'
ANY OTHER BRIGHT IDEAS?"

"AND THIS IS BELVEDERE'S TROPHY ROOM."

"OH, OH, I'M AFRAID TO ASK WHAT WENT WRONG AROUND HERE TODAY."

"YOU DECIDED TO PUT OUT A SIGN AND HAVE A **WHAT** SALE?"

"THAT MESSY STUFF YOU REMOVED FROM THE CRACKS IS CALLED CAULKING."

"COME BACK! NOBODY'S BLAMING YOU FOR IT!"

"AND THIS ONE COMES WITH SHOULDER STRAPS IN CASE YOU LIKE TAKING YOUR DOG CAMPING."

"THEY HAVE A VACANCY. WHERE'S BELVEDERE?"

" I JUST THOUGHT OF A PERFECT JOB FOR YOU....
A VENTRILOQUIST'S DUMMY. "

" I DIDN'T MEAN **THAT** RARE. "

" HE INSISTED ON A KING SIZE. "

" LET'S HOPE OUR GUESTS NEVER FIND OUT WHY
WE RAN OUT OF PUNCH SO EARLY. "

"I'VE SEEN LAZY DOG OWNERS BEFORE, BUT THIS BEATS ALL!"

I SAID NO DOGGIE TRICKS 'TIL AFTER DINNER."

"NEVER MIND WARMING UP. HIT HIM!"

"NOW THAT'S WHAT I CALL A RUM CAKE!"

"ORDINARILY HIS TRAPS AREN'T THIS ELABORATE."

"IF YOU'RE BORED, WE'LL JUST GO HOME."

"LET'S SEE YOU TOP THAT ONE!"

"WE ALMOST LET THAT ONE GET AWAY!"

"HE'S JUST FULL OF DOGGIE TRICKS TODAY."

"SO YOU FINALLY SPOTTED A RABBIT. BIG DEAL."

" HE WON'T SHARE LASSIE WITH ANYONE. "

"I SAID I'D FRY THE FISH, IF YOU DON'T MIND!"

"NOW DON'T WORRY. WE'LL GET HER CALMED DOWN IN NO TIME."

"GOOD GRIEF. IF YOU FIND THAT NEW FRENCH POODLE NEXT DOOR SO INTERESTING, WHY DON'T YOU JUST TROT OVER AND INTRODUCE YOURSELF."

"THIS MUST BE THE MINIATURE GOLF COURSE
HERE AT YOSEMITE PARK."

"HE'S CARRIED THE ART OF WATCH-DOGGING TO AN ALL-TIME ZENITH."

"SORRY."

"NO, THIS IS ORVILLE'S PH.D. — THAT'S BELVEDERE'S OBEDIENCE SCHOOL DIPLOMA."

"NO MORE FOR HIM."

© Field Enterprises, Inc., 1980

3-13

GEORGE RENSHAW

"I MIXED HIS PILLS IN WITH THE HAMBURGER. HE'LL NEVER KNOW THE DIFFERENCE."

GEORGE RENSHAW 1-1

"I THINK HE WAS REALLY OUT ON THE TOWN LAST NIGHT!"

"LOOK AT IT THIS WAY... IF YOUR LIFE WAS A T.V. SERIES, YOU WOULD HAVE BEEN CANCELLED."

"ALL RIGHT, CONFESS! WHO TOOK MY LIVERWURST?"

"THAT'S NOTHING. YOU SHOULD HAVE SEEN THEM CHASING LAST YEAR IN RIVER RAFTS."

"ANTIDISESTABLISHMENTARIANISM."

"WHAT'S THIS BILL FROM GRADY'S MARKET FOR NINETY-SEVEN POUNDS OF FILET MIGNON STEAK?"

"I'VE LOOKED HIGH AND LOW FOR THAT ELECTRIC BLANKET."

"DON'T WORRY ABOUT BELVEDERE. HE'S IN THE BACKYARD BURNING LEAVES LIKE YOU TOLD HIM TO."

"...THEN TOO, THERE ARE CERTAIN DRAWBACKS TO HAVING A FRISKY DOG FOR A PET."

"YOU'RE RIGHT. THERE'S NO RULE THAT SAYS HE CAN'T USE MAGNETS."

"NOW WHAT IN BLAZES HAPPENED TO MY LUNCH?"

"IF HE TRIES TO TAKE OVER AND RUN THINGS AROUND HERE, JUST LET US KNOW."

"FACE IT—MONEY TALKS AND YOURS IS SAYING GOODBYE!"

"CHI-CHI WANTS A PRETZEL...AND SHE WOULDN'T MIND A LITTLE SIP OF THAT BEER, TOO."

"A LITTLE UNORTHODOX, BUT HE'S A GREAT LITTLE RETRIEVER."

"IT WAS EASY. I TOLD HIM HE WAS THE FIRST DOG
IN HISTORY TO HAVE ACUPUNCTURE."

"MAKES ME WONDER.... WITH BELVEDERE LOOKING AFTER THINGS, WHAT WILL HOME LOOK LIKE WHEN WE RETURN?"

"DON'T LET HIM SHOP WITH ME AT THE BUTCHER'S ANYMORE. I ONLY WENT IN FOR A POUND OF HAMBURGER."

"GOOD GRIEF. I'M NOT EVEN AWAKE YET. WHAT IS IT NOW?"

"ALL RIGHT. SO I PUT EXTENDER IN YOUR HAMBURGER LAST NIGHT. SO WHAT ARE YOU GONNA DO ABOUT IT?"

"...AND STOP CALLING ME 'WARDEN'."

"I'LL SAY ONE THING—AT LEAST HE'S RUNNING AWAY FROM HOME IN STYLE."

"VERY GOOD. NOW TRY THE BOTTOM LINE."

NAT

4-27

" SOMETHING TELLS ME THIS AIN'T GONNA BE JUST
ANY ORDINARY ROUTINE DAY, BRINKLY. "

12-20

GEORGE
CRENSHAW

" IT'S YOUR RENEWAL NOTICE FROM DOGHOUSE AND GARDEN. "

"I THINK JEZEBEL KNOWS WE'VE BEEN TO THE FISH MARKET."

"ISN'T THAT CUTE? HE'S TRYING TO TELL US SOMETHING."

"REMEMBER WHEN HE USED TO JUST SCRATCH AT THE DOOR AND WHINE TO COME IN?"

"WE'VE GOT TO GET CHI CHI A BIRD CAGE."

" HE LIKES TO DO HIS BEGGING TRICK THE BEST. "

" WELL, YOU'RE OFF TO A GOOD START THIS MORNING. YOU'RE
NOT LISTED IN THE OBITUARY COLUMN. "

"WHY CAN'T HE JUST BARK AT PEDDLERS LIKE OTHER DOGS DO?"

"ORVILLE AND BELVEDERE SHOT IT ON A TIGER SHOOT.
THEY WERE RIDING IT AT THE TIME."

"WHAT IN HEAVEN'S NAME HAS HE BUILT?!"

"VERY NICE, BUT DO YOU REALIZE IT'S THE THIRD ONE OF THOSE SIGNS HE SOLD YOU THIS WEEK?!"

" WHY DIDN'T YOU OPEN THE DOOR? I TOLD YOU HE WANTS IN. "

10-26

"WHY CAN'T HE JUST FETCH THE PAPER LIKE OTHER DOGS DO?"

11-4

"THAT MUST BE JUST ABOUT THE **HIGHEST** 'C' SHE'S EVER REACHED."

"WELL, HOW'S HE DOING? HAS HE CAPTURED MY LIKENESS?"

"OH, ALL RIGHT. YOU CAN TOSS THE SALAD."

"WELL, HOW ABOUT THAT? A BIRTHDAY PRESENT FROM BELVEDERE. AND I THOUGHT HE WAS MAD AT ME ABOUT SOMETHING."

"NOW WHO TOOK THE LEGS OFF MY FAVORITE ROCKER?"

"I SEE YOU'VE BEEN ASSIGNED TO BELVEDERE'S BLOCK."

"MAN! IT SURE WAS DARK WHEN WE PITCHED CAMP LAST NIGHT."

"HE SAYS IT'S A PICTURE OF A COAL MINER CHASING A BLACK CAT THROUGH A TRAIN TUNNEL ON A DARK NIGHT."

"MY PIZZA IS NOT TOUGH. YOU HAPPEN TO BE EATING THE CORK PLACE-MAT!"

"NOW I'VE SEEN EVERYTHING!"

"GIVE IT UP. YOU'LL NEVER GET IN THE LAST WORD."

2-15

© Field Enterprises, Inc., 1960

"I HOPE BELVEDERE GOT ALONG WITH HIS NEW SITTER."

2-21

GEORGE RENSHAW

"WELL, HERE IT IS. I FOUND MY MEERSCHAUM PIPE, PLUS TWO CASES OF BRANDY, A TROMBONE, AND TWELVE CAT SCALPS."

"I'M UP! I'M UP! I'M UP! **I'M UP!** I'M UP!"

"WE'RE READY TO PUSH OFF, OLD BUDDY. NOW, WHERE'S THE SADDLE?"

"I DON'T BELIEVE IT EITHER."

" I THINK HE'S IN A GOOD MOOD THIS MORNING.
HE JUST SAID, 'GDZL NXLIPHTT. "

" THIS LOOKS LIKE A GOOD SPOT. "

"NO DOUBT HE WAS WONDERING WHERE HE LEFT HIS CLOTHES."

"YOUR MAKE-IT-YOURSELF DOGHOUSE IS HERE."

"IT'S A NEW CHOW IN GARBAGE PAIL CANS.
DOGS LOVE IT."

"MIDGE! COME QUICK! THIS NEW HAIR TONIC IS MIRACULOUS!"

"HOW ARE YOU MAKING OUT WITH THAT WHITE SPOTTED POOCH, DOCTOR?"

"I THOUGHT I PUT YOU OUT FOR THE NIGHT."

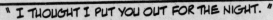

© Field Enterprises, Inc., 1980

"I TARPED OVER THE POOL FOR THE WINTER. NOW BELVEDERE HAS THE BIGGEST WATER BED IN THE COUNTY."

1-25

GEORGE RENSHAW

"HIS FOOD BOWL MUST BE EMPTY."

1-15

GEORGE RENSHAW

"OH, COME NOW, HARGRAVES...ALL OBEDIENCE SCHOOL TRAINERS HAVE THEIR BAD DAYS."

GEORGE RENSHAW

© Field Enterprises, Inc., 198

"MY STEAK SEEMED A LITTLE TOUGH SO YOU PRE-CHEWED IT

" MIGHT AS WELL GET IT OVER WITH. GO AHEAD, ASK HIM TO SPEAK. "

"YOU SHOULD NEVER HAVE TAUGHT HIM TO FETCH THE PAPER."

"WHY DIDN'T YOU JUST SKIP THE PART ABOUT '4 AND 20 BLACKBIRDS BAKED INTO A PIE'?!"

"DOES HE HAVE TO BRING THAT ESKIMO DOG IN THE HOUSE?!"

"IT'S NOT YOUR MOTHER WHO'S PAYING THE $5.95, PLUS TAX, FOR THREE MINUTES OF 'O SOLE MIO'!"

"HE'S PROBABLY THE LAZIEST WATCHDOG IN THE WORLD!"

"AND IF BELVEDERE GIVES YOU ANY TROUBLE, JUST GIVE US A CALL."

"WE'D BETTER CHECK THE RULEBOOK ON THIS."

" HE CAUGHT EVERY CAT IN OUR NEIGHBORHOOD.
NOW HE'S AFTER CATFISH. "

" NOW JUST A MINUTE THERE ! "

"MAYBE IF YOU JUST GAVE HER YOUR AUTOGRAPH SHE'D GO AWAY."

"I'M THIRSTY!"

"DON'T LIE TO ME. YOU'VE GOTTEN INTO MY GARDEN SEEDS AGAIN, HAVEN'T YOU?"

"I STILL SAY HIS ART COLLECTION LEAVES A LOT TO BE DESIRED."

"LOOK AT IT THIS WAY.... YOU'RE ONLY ONE TEN-MILLIONTH AS MUCH IN DEBT AS THE FEDERAL GOVERNMENT."

"LOOK...I SAID I'D TEACH YOU POLO NEXT WEEK."

"YOU MIGHT SAY HE HAS A SPLIT PERSONALITY. SOMETIMES HE'S ABSOLUTELY RAVENOUS AND OTHER TIMES HE'S JUST PLAIN STARVED."

" I THINK ALL HE WANTS IS A LITTLE ATTENTION."

"NONSENSE. WHATEVER MAKES YOU THINK THIS IS BIGFOOT COUNTRY?"

"I THINK HE LIKES HIS NEW HELICOPTER!"

"SO SHE CAN'T STAND MY SMELLY PIPES. WHAT DO I CARE WHAT A CAT THINKS."

"TALK ABOUT A PAMPERED CAT."

" IN SOME PARTS OF THE WORLD, WHOLE VILLAGES
COULD LIVE ON HIS FOOD INTAKE. "

" SHE'S SO SENSITIVE DURING MOLTING SEASON. "

"IT'S THE HYENA AT THE ZOO. HE FINALLY FOUND SOMEONE TO LAUGH AT HIS CORNY JOKES."

"IT'S JUST BELVEDERE CHASING A CAT."

"KEEP YOUR EYES AND EARS OPEN. THE ANACONDA IS KNOWN TO BE VERY TRICKY."

"LOOK!...DON'T INTERRUPT WHILE I'M BUTTING IN!"

"IT LOOKS LIKE HE SPENT ANOTHER NIGHT TOSSING AND TURNING!"

"A POT OF BONES?"

"WHAT A NIGHTMARE! I DREAMED BELVEDERE WAS CLONED!"

©Field Enterprises, Inc., 1981

"I SAID, JUST SERVE THEM. NEVER MIND THE FANFARE!"

"NO, YOU CANNOT HIRE A CLEANING SERVICE TO COME IN ONCE A WEEK."

"OH, ALL RIGHT THEN! I'LL TAKE YOU ICE SKATING!"

"TWO BATS BROUGHT HER HOME AT DAWN
AND PUT HER TO BED."

"A *LIVER* MILKSHAKE??"

"BELVEDERE WON'T BE ANY TROUBLE. HE BROUGHT SOME OF HIS PLAY THINGS."

"YES, THEY CLAIM A CAT ALWAYS LANDS ON ITS FEET, WHY?"

"A GRAPE-EATING COW? I WONDERED WHERE HE WAS GETTING ALL THAT WINE."

"ALL RIGHT! I'M COMING! I'M COMING!"

"ALL RIGHT, GO AHEAD AND WRITE ANN LANDERS AND YOUR CONGRESSMAN. THERE'LL BE NO FREE BONES TODAY."

"HE'S PUTTING IN A BONE CELLAR."

"A WIENERSICLE FOR DOGS?"

"THAT DOES IT! TOMORROW, OUT SHE GOES!"

"WE'RE GETTING YOU A NEW BIRD CAGE NEXT MONTH. NOW STOP YOUR COMPLAINING!"

"I SAY WE LET HIM GO. HE'S CALLING F. LEE BAILEY."

"OH, STOP COMPLAINING AND START YOUR RACE. HE'S GIVING YOU A FAIR HANDICAP, ISN'T HE?"

"OH, ALL RIGHT. SHOW ME YOUR LEVITATION TRICK."

© Field Enterprises, Inc., 1981

GEORGE CRENSHAW

1-9

"HEY, GANG — THAT'S NOT THE THREE STOOGES YOU'RE WATCHING. I REPLACED THE PICTURE TUBE WITH A MIRROR."

NAT

11-19

" NOW WAS THAT NICE? I ASKED YOU TO **HAND** ME MY 4 IRON. "

" I'M NOT SURE, BUT I THINK I SAW HIM PUT
AN OLIVE IN IT. "

" WAS IT BELVEDERE AGAIN ? "

"I DON'T BELIEVE IT!"

" OH, COME NOW. MY BARBEQUED STEAKS AREN'T **THAT** TOUGH. "

"OF COURSE, THERE ARE CERTAIN DRAWBACKS TO VACATIONING ON A HOUSEBOAT."

"IF MY SMOKING BOTHERS YOU, WHY DON'T YOU JUST SAY SO."

"... AND FROM NOW ON REMEMBER THAT 'TAKING THE BULL BY THE HORNS' IS JUST A FIGURE OF SPEECH."

"YEA, I LIKE OX-TAIL SOUP. WHY?"

"IT LOOKS LIKE A WHITE SPOTTED DOG WHO HAS A HALF-NELSON ON A OVERSIZED BULL MOOSE."

"THIS LOOKS LIKE AS GOOD A PLACE AS ANY."

"I DON'T MIND LETTING YOU DRIVE, BUT COULDN'T YOU HAVE THOUGHT OF A BETTER WAY TO AVOID ALL THE TRAFFIC?"

"HE'S NOT JUST ANY ORDINARY HUNTING DOG."

" I SUPPOSE TOMORROW THEY'LL BE CHASING
ON SKATE BOARDS. "

" HE LOVES TO GIVE A FRIEND A HELPING HAND. "

" MAYBE IF YOU USED JUMPER CABLES YOU COULD GET HIM STARTED. "

" I TOLD YOU HE'S A NATURAL BORN LEADER! "

"MAYBE WE OUGHT TO JUST SKIP HIS DISTEMPER SHOT THIS FALL."

"YOU WEREN'T KIDDING! HE IS TRICKY!"

"ALL RIGHT, WHERE ARE THEY? FOUR OF MY GOLF CLUB COVERS ARE MISSING!"

"THERE ARE FEW FATHERS OF HIS CALIBER."

"FIRST WE TAUGHT HIM TO BRING IN THE PAPER, AND NOW HE HAS HIS OWN PAPER ROUTE."

"YOU SAY I'M OVERDRAWN — I SAY YOU'RE UNDERDEPOSITED!"

"REMEMBER THE GOOD OLD DAYS WHEN HE USED TO JUST **RETRIEVE** THE MORNING PAPER?"

"HE'S THE ONLY DOG IN TOWN WITH HIS OWN SAFETY DEPOSIT BOX."

"HE MUST BE AROUND THERE SOMEWHERE, MR. BUTLER.
HE ALWAYS CATCHES THE 8:15 BUS."

"OK! OK! IT'S FEEDING TIME!"

"NOW, MRS. HOOPER, TELL THE COURT WHAT HAPPENED WHEN YOU AND THE NEIGHBOR'S DOG ARGUED OVER THE ELECTRIC HEDGE CLIPPERS."

BOOM!

" YOU DIDN'T HAVE TO TAKE WHAT BELVEDERE
SAID SO LITERALLY, DEAR. "

"WHY CAN'T THEY JUST HIDE UNDER THE BED LIKE OTHER PETS DO?"

"JUST ONCE I WISH WE COULD GET AWAY FOR A FEW DAYS WITHOUT A SCENE."

"HOW WELL DID YOU SAY YOU KNEW THESE WOODS?"

"CAN'T YOU THINK OF SOME EASIER
WAY TO GIVE UP SMOKING ?!"

"YOU GUIDED US TO THIS POINT. NOW WHAT ?"

"NOW TRY ONCE MORE, AND REMEMBER, — IT'S CLANG
BEFORE BANG EXCEPT AFTER CLANK."

"YOU KNOW HE WON'T EAT WITHOUT VIOLIN MUSIC."

"THEY ALWAYS STOP FOR TRANQUILIZERS BEFORE DRIVING UP BELVEDERE'S BLOCK."

"THERE! I TOLD YOU HE WAS RUNNING AWAY FROM HOME!"

"WE MADE THEM FOR YOU, DEAR. THEY'RE FOR SKIERS WHO DON'T KNOW WHETHER THEY'RE COMING OR GOING. "

"HE ABSOLUTELY INSISTED ON A PENTHOUSE. "

"I KNOW HE WAS A NAUGHTY DOGGIE, BUT DON'T YOU THINK DEPRIVING HIM OF WORCESTERSHIRE SAUCE FOR HIS FILET MIGNON STEAK IS RATHER SEVERE PUNISHMENT, DEAR?"

"WHY CAN'T HE USE AN ICE PACK LIKE EVERYBODY ELSE?"

"NOW TELL HIM HOW MUCH THE CITY ZOO SUED FOR AFTER YOU SHOT IT."

" WATCH OUT FOR THE..."

" MAYBE IT'S THE PROPYLENE GLYCOL HE DOESN'T CARE FOR. "

" HE'S REALLY QUITE GOOD ON CEILINGS "

"I THINK HE'S GOT IT CONNECTED TO THE HOT WATER HEATER!"

"HE TALKS THEM INTO SURRENDERING."

" WELL, HERE WE ARE AT YOUR SECRET FISHING SPOT. NOW WHERE ARE ALL THE WHOPPERS? "

" YOU HAVE TO ADMIRE HIS EQUANIMITY UNDER PRESSURE. "

" A PLAIN ORDINARY MOOSE CALL ISN'T GOOD ENOUGH FOR HIM. IT'S GOTTA BE IN STEREO. "

" HAVE YOU BEEN DRINKING FROM MY THERMOS ? "

"IT SAYS, 'DEAR FATSO!'...I THINK HE'S WRITING A LETTER TO SANTA CLAUS."

"SOME DOGS HAVE IT, AND SOME DON'T."

"I DON'T CARE IF SHE IS AN ALASKAN HUSKY, AND IF YOU ARE THE FATHER. I WON'T HAVE THAT NUTTY DOGHOUSE IN MY YARD!"

"FIRST HE STARTED CHASING CARS, THEN AIRPLANES—
NOW IT'S HELICOPTERS."

"SO HE BOUGHT SOMETHING AT A GARAGE SALE. SO WHAT?"

"I THINK HE'S GETTING READY TO TELL YOU
THE NAUGHTY THING HE DID TODAY."

"I BELIEVE HE'S BEGINNING TO CATCH ON."

" OH, DEAR — YOU SHOULD HAVE TOLD MISS CRUMP
THAT'S BELVEDERE'S CHAIR. "

" NOW, WHAT DID I TELL YOU ABOUT DOUBLE PARKING ? "

"HEH, HEH, HEH! MY NEW LOCK ON THE REFRIGERATOR PUT A STOP TO YOUR MIDNIGHT SNACK SNITCHING, DIDN'T IT, SMARTY!"

"I TOLD YOU TO KEEP AN EYE ON HIM TILL THE GUESTS ARRIVED!"

"JUST WHAT DID YOU TELL THE FOOD AND DRUG ADMINISTRATION ABOUT MY COOKING?"

"CAN'T YOU BE SERIOUS FOR JUST ONE MINUTE?"

"TAKE YOUR TIME. WE'D LIKE A COUPLE
OF HOURS SHOPPING IN PEACE."

"DO TWO PAIRS OF ONES BEAT ANYTHING?"

"WHAT A PHONY... THERE'S NO CLOTHESLINE."

© Field Enterprises, Inc., 1979

12-3

"ALL RIGHT. ALL RIGHT. I WON'T PUT ANYMORE HAMBURGER EXTENDER IN YOUR GROUND CHUCK."

GEORGE RENSHAW

© Field Enterprises, Inc., 1979

11-26

GEORGE RENSHAW

"WOULDN'T IT BE WONDERFUL IF SOMEONE WOULD INVENT A STRAW THAT COULD FILTER OUT THE CALORIES?"

"ACT NONCHALANT."

"YOU INVENTED A NEW CUCKOO CLOCK? HOW DOES IT WORK?"

"YOU FED HIM THAT FOR LUNCH, REMEMBER?"

"GOOD GRIEF, I JUST ASKED FOR A LITTLE DINNER MUSIC. CAN'T HE PLAY **ANYTHING** BUT THE 'ANVIL CHORUS'?"

"I ACCIDENTALLY SAID **HAMBURGER**."

"OH DEAR, MR. DEKKER. YOU SHOULD NEVER HAVE ASKED HIM TO SHAKE."

"I HEARD IT WAS AN ELECTION BET."

" YOU SHOULD HAVE KNOWN BETTER THAN
TO ASK HIM TO GIVE YOU A PUSH. "

" LASSIE SHOW. "

"THEY HAVE MORE FUN ON A VACATION!"

"GUESS IT'S JUST ONE OF THOSE DAYS."

"I SUPPOSE WE SHOULD FEEL PROUD. AFTER ALL, NOT MANY DOGS TODAY HAVE A MECHANICAL HOLE DIGGER."

"IT'S HIS OWN ARRANGEMENT OF *HOLD THAT TIGER.*"

"WHY CAN'T HE JUST *NIP* AT THEIR PANTS LIKE OTHER DOGS DO?"

"THAT'S RIGHT. I SAID HURRY AND WAKE HIM UP.
I DON'T CARE *HOW*."

"I DUNNO, HE WAS RIGHT HERE A MOMENT AGO!"

"DON'T ASK ME. HE PUTS IN ONE BONE AND OUT COMES TEN."

"JUST CARRY THE BAG, I'LL DO THE SWINGING!"

"KEEP YOUR EARS OPEN. THE KLONDIKE MOOSE
CAN SOMETIMES BE VERY SNEAKY!"

"ALL RIGHT. WHO PUT THE BUBBLE GUM IN MY TUBA?"

"YOU'LL HAVE TO ADMIT IT, REVEREND — HIS PLAYING DEAD ACT IS QUITE ORIGINAL."

"NOT AGAIN ?!!"

4-16

"I SHOULD HAVE KNOWN BETTER THAN TO ASK YOU TO HELP ME FIX A SIMPLE BATHROOM LEAK."

4-17

GEORGE CRENSHAW

"HE LOVES SHISH KABOB."

"DON'T BE RIDICULOUS. THERE AREN'T ANY DOGFISH FOR MILES AROUND."

"HOW LONG HAS IT BEEN SINCE A CRUMB FELL ALL THE WAY TO THE FLOOR?"

12-13

GEORGE RENSHAW

12-16

"I WONDER IF BELVEDERE LIKED MY MEATBALLS?"

GEORGE RENSHAW

"WE'RE IN LUCK. THAT PESTY POOCH DOESN'T SEEM TO BE AROUND TONIGHT."

"WHERE'S MY NEW PIPE?"

"YOU HAD TO PROMISE TO TAKE HIM FISHING BRIGHT
AND EARLY THIS MORNING!"

"THAT IS **NOT** HOW WE DRESS A CHRISTMAS TREE!"

"WHEN HE'S A GOOD DOGGIE ALL DAY, I LET HIM LOOK UNINTERRUPTED FOR TWENTY MINUTES."

"PERHAPS WE SHOULD TRY TO GET HIM INTERESTED IN MUSIC."

" OH, STOP COMPLAINING. HE'S GIVING YOU A FAIR HANDICAP, ISN'T HE ? "

"WE CAN ALWAYS HOPE FOR A POWER FAILURE."

" LOOK! WE'LL EITHER PLAY ACCORDING TO HOYLE, OR NOT AT ALL ! "

" NO, NO, STUPID. THAT'S NOT HOW IT'S DONE ! "

"IT'S BELVEDERE'S OBEDIENCE SCHOOL.
HE'S ORGANIZED A CAMPUS RIOT!"

"GUESS WHAT? CHI-CHI HAS LEARNED TO USE THE TELEPHONE."

"MAYBE WE SHOULD NEVER HAVE TOLD HIM
HE'S A MIXTURE OF GERMAN SHEPHERD,
ALASKAN HUSKY, SPITZ, AND MEXICAN CHIHUAHUA."

"HE HATES THE SMELL OF CIGAR SMOKE."

"GOOD HEAVENS, ORVILLE— WHY DON'T YOU JUST
TAKE HIM FOR A TROT AND GET IT OVER WITH ?!"

"HE TAKES ALL THE SPORT OUT OF EVERYTHING."

" OH, COME NOW -- CERTAINLY YOU DON'T EXPECT ME TO
BELIEVE IN A LOT OF NUTTY WITCHCRAFT, DO YOU ? "

" BETTER SKIP BELVEDERE THIS NEXT ROUND, DEAR. "

"LOOSELY TRANSLATED, MRS. FLOOGLE, HE SAID YOUR CUISINE IS NOT PARTICULARLY HAUTE."

"IT'S DELICIOUS. WHAT DID YOU USE FOR MORTAR?"

: "PERHAPS YOU'D ALSO LIKE TO CHECK OVER MY
BLUEPRINTS AND BUILDER'S PERMIT?"

"NEVER MIND THE FLYSWATTER, DEAR."

"MAYBE HE NEEDS A VACATION – LIKE A ONE-WAY TRIP TO THE BERMUDA TRIANGLE."

"WHO'S BEEN READING MY MAGIC BOOK?"

"CLOSEST THEY'VE COME TO CATCHING HIM THIS WEEK."

"NOW THERE'S A SIGHT YOU SELDOM SEE."

"DON'T LAUGH. HE'S GOT A DOUBLE MIXTURE OF 'SUPER-RAPID-QUICK-GROW' IN THAT WATERING CAN."

"VISITING HOURS ARE OVER."

"GO ON - YOU DUG A HOLE UNDER THE HOUSE TO BURY YOUR BONE, AND **WHAT** HAPPENED?"

"WHY CAN'T HE JUST **WALK** IN HIS SLEEP?"

" I UNDERSTAND IT ALSO HAS A SAUNA, WINE CELLAR, WET BAR AND JACUZZI."

" SURPRISE, DEAR. BELVEDERE OILED THE GARAGE DOOR."

"SOMEBODY HAS TO EAT IT, OR HE WON'T GET HIS OBEDIENCE SCHOOL MERIT BADGE."

"BATTLE STATIONS!"

"HE DIDN'T SAY YOUR MEAT PATTIES WERE TOUGH, DEAR. HE MERELY ASKED FOR A HAMMER AND CHISEL."

"NOW THERE'S A PAINTING THAT REALLY *SAYS* SOMETHING!"

"VERY NICE, BUT WE'RE NOT INTERESTED IN HANGING YOUR BABY PICTURE OVER THE MANTEL."

"THE NEIGHBORS SAID BELVEDERE'S BEEN HANGING AROUND THE RACE TRACK. DID YOU EVER HEAR OF ANYTHING SO RIDICULOUS?"

"EXCUSE THE COMMOTION. ORVILLE IS TEACHING BELVEDERE ALL ABOUT JUDO."

"DON'T LOOK SO FRUSTRATED. YOU DON'T HAVE TO BURY A BONE EVERY TIME YOU SEE A HOLE."

"YOU WANT YOUR STEAK BURNT OR WELL-BURNT?"

"OH, COME NOW, FINNEGAN — HE CAN'T BE *THAT* NAUGHTY A DOGGIE!"

"OH, WHAT IS IT?"

" BELVEDERE TOLD THE MOVERS TO DELIVER MY NEW PIANO **WHERE ?** "

" I TOLD YOU TO SIP IT. "

"I'VE NEVER SEEN HIM BEFORE EITHER!"

"YOU SHOULD KNOW BETTER THAN TO FEED HIM AT THE TABLE."

"I DON'T KNOW WHERE HE CAME FROM EITHER, BUT GET HIM OUTA HERE!"

"YOU DON'T SEE MANY HOMES THESE DAYS WITH A PET GIRAFFE."

"THERE'S NO MISTAKE.
THE ORDER CAME FROM THIS HOUSE."

"THIS SHOULD SETTLE THE QUESTION OF WHOSE CHAIR IT IS."

"A BLINDFOLD AND A LAST CIGARETTE?"

"IT'S JUST UNTIL WE CATCH THIS BELVEDERE MUTT.
THEN YOU CAN GO BACK TO NORMAL DUTY."

"I HOPE YOU DISCIPLINED BELVEDERE FOR BEING NAUGHTY THIS MORNING. DEAR?...WHERE ARE YOU, DEAR?..."

" IT'S THE ONE PLEASURE I ALLOW HIM WHEN HE HELPS ME SHOP. "

" DID YOU HAVE TO ORDER IN FRENCH? "

" YOU SORT OF HAVE TO ADMIRE HIS DIRECT
NO-NONSENSE APPROACH TO HOUSEWORK. "

" NEVER TELL AN ELEPHANT JOKE TO AN ELEPHANT! "

"NO, I DO NOT THINK CROSSING A KUMQUAT TREE WITH A RUBBER TREE WILL GROW GOLF BALLS."

"HE'S BEEN ACTING LIKE THAT EVER SINCE HIS FRENCH POODLE JILTED HIM."

"WELL, HURRY IT UP, OLD BUDDY. I'M WAITING
FOR THE CHEF'S SURPRISE."

"HOLD IT RIGHT THERE!"

" FIRST, LET ME EXPLAIN THE RULES... "

"NOW THAT'S WHAT I CALL ONE **SCARED** SNAKE!"

"DON'T DRINK ANY OF HIS SILLY CONCOCTIONS, DEAR, THEY COULD HAVE SIDE EFFECTS."

"A FINE SPOTTER YOU TURNED OUT TO BE!"

" HOW DID BELVEDERE LIKE THAT NEW DOG FOOD WE BOUGHT, DEAR? "

"HIS CHASING CARS DOESN'T BOTHER ME. IT'S WHEN HE BRINGS THEM HOME AND BURIES THEM!"

"HE'S AROUND HERE SOMEPLACE. I KNOW IT!"

"STOP WORRYING, YOU TWO. IT SAYS HERE IN THE HANDBOOK THAT THE GREAT HORNED OWL CANNOT CARRY OFF ANYTHING HEAVIER THAN A LARGE SQUIRREL."

"THAT'S RIGHT. I ASKED BELVEDERE TO CLEAR THE TABLE."

"I'M NOT REALLY COMPLAINING, BUT WHY DOES THE *LASSIE* SHOW AND HIS WALK PERIOD HAVE TO BE AT THE SAME TIME?"

"HAS ANYONE SEEN MY SAXOPHONE?"

"WELL, JUST WHAT *DID* YOU EXPECT A MARTIAN TO LOOK LIKE?"

" IT KEEPS HIM HAPPY ON RAINY DAYS. "

BELVEDERE

A Tor Book

Published by Tom Doherty Associates, 8-10 W. 36th St., New York City, N.Y. 10018

First printing, February 1983

ISBN: 523-49027-5

Printed in the United States of America

Distributed by Pinnacle Books, 1430 Broadway, New York, N.Y. 10018

BELVEDERE

by

George Crenshaw

A TOM DOHERTY ASSOCIATES BOOK